An Unexpected Affair

THE DR. CAGE CHRONICLES:
MEMOIRS OF A SEX THERAPIST

An Unexpected Affair

GRAYSON ACE

4 Horsemen
Publications, Inc.

An Unexpected Affair
Copyright © 2022 Grayson Ace. All rights reserved.

4 Horsemen Publications, Inc.
1497 Main St. Suite 169
Dunedin, FL 34698
4horsemenpublications.com
info@4horsemenpublications.com

Editor Tilda M. Cooke

Library of Congress Control Number: 2022939537

Print ISBN: 978-1-64450-635-6
Ebook ISBN: 978-1-64450-633-2
Audio ISBN: 978-1-64450-634-9

Chapter 1

THE RETURN OF PETE

After my whirlwind trip to Europe, I knew I needed to take a break for a little bit. A vacation from my vacation. I couldn't stop thinking about the men that I was with during my adventure and couldn't believe that I had actually found the sex house from the porno that I had been jerking off to for years. This was certainly a trip that I would never forget, and one that I was already looking forward to repeating.

Rocky had been handling the clinic for me while I was on vacation, and I was pretty surprised to see how many appointments he had booked. It made me wish I had taken more time on my vacation because it was starting to look like I wasn't going to have much of a social life anytime soon with the number of clients I was seeing. I was starting to consider expanding and actually hiring another therapist because there was no way I was going to be able to maintain this client base on my own.

My first day back at the office was pretty hectic. Rocky had booked me six appointments, which I was a little pissed about because he knew I was just returning from Europe. I looked at the calendar and saw that Pete was my first client of the day. I sent Rocky a text and told him to cancel my following two appointments because I knew I was going to need some extra time with Pete.

Pete was the guy who randomly yelled "see you next week" at the mall. He came in for his first appointment trying to figure out if he was a top or a bottom. I fucked him so good during his first appointment, and he wanted to flip at one point, but his hole was so warm and wet that I wasn't willing to pull out. So I knew he'd be coming back to take a turn at my ass.

Pete walked into my office with a giant smile on his face. He was wearing gym shorts and a tank top, and it was obvious that he didn't have any underwear on because I could see his monster dangling down and pointing out. We walked back to the therapy room and sat down on the couch. I grabbed my notebook and told him to tell me what kind of progress he had made since our last appointment.

Well, I really haven't made much progress. Actually, I haven't made any at all. I've hooked up with a few guys since my last appointment, but I bottomed for all of them. With one of them, I was really horned up and wanted him to get on top of me and ride me, but I got nervous and didn't ask. I'm probably just destined to be a bottom for the rest of my life because I'm really not sure how to take charge.

As I was taking my notes, I laughed internally about his comment of not knowing how to take charge. Pete had big dick energy—he needed to learn how to use it to his advantage.

"Here's what we are going to do, Pete. You're going to fuck me. You're going to make all the moves. The ball is in your court." I tossed my notebook down on the floor and looked at him. I could tell he was a bit confused and not sure what to do.

"Go ahead. Make your move."

He crawled toward me on the couch, turning my body so that my head was on the armrest and legs on the couch and got on top of me. He leaned down and started kissing me, rubbing his body against mine. He was a damn good kisser, and even with my pants on, I could feel his dick dangling between my legs. He unbuttoned my shirt and started sucking on my nipples, and I felt his hand move down my chest to my cock. He got up and pulled my pants off, dropping back down and swallowing my already hard cock. I held on tight to the back of his head as it bobbed up and down, dropping my cock out of his mouth and moving down toward my balls. I started stroking my dick as he was sucking on my balls before coming back up and teasing the head.

He grabbed onto the back of my legs and lifted them above his shoulders, diving his face right into my hole. I started squirming as his tongue went around and inside, making my ass completely wet. He sucked on his finger and shoved it in, fucking my hole with it while he licked around the edges. I was completely thrown off that he was able to go from completely not knowing what to do to entirely taking charge of the situation. At this point, I was ready for him to start pounding my ass, but this was his event to manage.

He put my legs back down and then stood up, ripping off his tank top and dropping his shorts to the ground. His hard cock immediately bounced up, and he came over to the side of the couch and shove it right into my face. I leaned on my side and grabbed onto the base, allowing him to completely gag me with his monster. He grabbed onto the back of my head and started fucking my mouth, pulling it out and shoving it completely back in. He was finally showing me the big dick energy that he really had.

After a few minutes of gagging on his dick, he practically picked me up and flipped me onto my stomach, my head leaning on the armrest. He got behind me and spread my legs apart, spitting on my hole and on his cock to get it nice and wet. I forgot to grab the lube from my drawer before the session, but this guy was a natural. I grabbed onto my ass cheeks and spread them apart as he guided his head toward me. He had 10 inches to offer me, and I wanted all of it. He slid his cock inside of me, and I was surprised how smoothly it went in. Once I felt that he was completely inside of me, I reached around and grabbed onto his hips, holding him against me to give myself a minute to adjust. He laid his chest against my back and started kissing on my neck, and I felt him slowly start to thrust his hips back and forth.

He went slow for a few moments and then pushed himself off of me, grabbing onto my hips and pulling me back to him in the doggy position. He started thrusting his cock faster and harder, and after a minute was completely owning my ass. This is exactly what I wanted him to do, and even more so, I could tell was exactly what he wanted.

He must have fucked me like this for a solid five or six minutes before pulling his cock out and flipping me back over on my back. He lifted my legs over his shoulders and slid his tool back inside of me, stroking my cock at the same rhythm he was fucking me. I could feel that he was starting to tense up and knew he wasn't going to last much longer, so I pushed him out of me and told him to sit down so I could ride him. I lowered myself onto his cock and started bouncing as fast and as hard as I could until he let out a loud scream, and I could feel him unleashing his batter deep inside of me.

I kept riding him while I was stroking my cock, milking him for every last drop I could get. He grabbed onto my hips and pulled me off of him and toward his face, and just as I started shooting my load, he opened up his mouth and pulled my hips toward him so he could start sucking my dick. I was surprised that he wanted it in his mouth but certainly wasn't disappointed. He bobbed his head back and forth until there was nothing left to pull out of me. I sat back down on his lap and kept making out with him for a few more minutes before standing up to put my clothes back on.

"Well, Pete. How did that feel?"

Honestly Doc, I had no clue that I had this side to me. I never would have imagined that I had this much strength inside of me. I think I might be a top!

Although I never enjoyed hearing those words, as I personally believe that everyone should be verse, I was happy to have made some progress.

See you next week!

Apparently, Pete wanted to come back for some more.

Chapter 2

TONY & NICK

*A*fter my session with Pete, I had Rocky cancel the rest of my appointments for the day. I felt bad always cancelling on my clients, but not matter how much I cancelled, I never lost anyone. It felt like people were willing to wait as long as it would take to experience my forward-thinking therapy.

I was still doing some daydreaming about my trip to Europe, but it also made me a little sad because, although the crazy adventures were thrilling, they weren't necessary fulfilling. And as much fun as a sex-filled European trip was, a sex-filled European trip with one person

10

would be even better. I still couldn't believe that I had a chance encounter with Nick in the airport before even leaving for Europe. It really was a shame that he was so messed up because he was someone that I could see myself with, although it will never happen.

As I was headed to the office the next morning, Rocky texted me and told me that I only had one appointment scheduled for the day. I was a little pissed because I was falling behind and needed to get so many of my clients rescheduled. When I arrived and looked at the calendar, I realized why he had freed up my day.

I was meeting with Tony and Nick.

I had completely forgotten that I told Tony to make another appointment and to bring Nick with him. I wonder if he had followed the instructions that I had given to him.

They arrived at my office a few minutes later, and as always, Nick and I didn't let on that we knew each other. I shook both of their hands and told Nick to wait in the lobby while I had a chat with Tony.

"So Tony, how have things been since the last time you were here? Did you take my advice?"

Well, sort of. So, I did what you told me. While we were getting ready for the show, Nick was stroking his dick to get fluffed up for the show—it's a normal thing to do before we go on. I walked over to him and asked if I could give him a hand, and I dropped down in front of him and started sucking on his cock. But ... I couldn't stop. Once I started, I just kept going, and he grabbed onto the back of my head and gagged me as he busted his nut. I had every intention of stopping, but I didn't want to. His load went completely down my throat, and then he just walked away and went on stage to perform.

I was actually surprised that he had made the move. But then I realized that Nick fucked me the same night, which was even more reassuring for me why Nick and I could never be together.

"What happened after that night?"

Nothing. Nothing has happened. I've asked him to hang out a few times, but our schedules never align. I'm in love with him, but I'm realizing he doesn't feel the same way about me. I really just want one chance to be with him, and if that means including you, then I don't care. I just want him.

I was a bit thrown off when he said including me. Did he know my and Nick's history? Or was he saying it more generally?

"Okay Tony, let's get Nick in here and see what we can work out."

I went up to the front office and told Nick to follow me back. I normally wouldn't do this, but I gave Nick a quick run-down of what was going to happen.

"Look, Nick. Tony is in love with you. He knows you don't feel the same, but he just wants a chance to hook up with you."

Nick laughed. "If he wanted to fuck, he didn't need to bring me here to do it. People fuck in the fitting rooms all the time. He already sucked my dick. He should have just asked."

I grinned at him and told him that we were going to make it happen today.

We walked back into the office, and Nick sat down on the couch next to Tony. "Okay, so here's what we're going to do. You both know the kind of therapy sessions I offer here, and I'm just going to be frank and to the point. Nick, Tony wants to fuck, and he invited you here so that the three of us would mess around together. So that's what we're going to do today."

I sat down on the couch and pulled Tony over toward me and had him straddle my lap. I pulled his head to mine and started making out with him. He was a really great kisser, and we immediately pulled each other's shirts off. He started kissing and sucking on my neck, then kissed his way to my nipples. He bit them a little bit and then made his way down my chest toward my dick. He looked up at me and was kissing my stomach while he was rubbing his hand on my dick through my pants.

Tony started unbuttoning my jeans and opened them just enough to pull my dick out. I was semi-hard at this point, and he started slowly licking the head of my penis. He would lick the tip of it, then twirl his tongue around it a little bit before finally swallowing the entire thing. Nick was sitting next to us with his cock pulled out, stroking it while he watched us. He reached over and put his hand on the back of Tony's head as he bobbed up and down on my tool. I could tell that Nick was enjoying watching Tony blow me.

Nick leaned over and started kissing me, and after a few minutes, Tony moved over to start working on his dick. Nick leaned back on the couch and put his hands behind his head and let Tony do all the work. Nick completely pulled Tony's shorts off, exposing the rest of him. He wasn't gentle with him like he was with me, and he just went to town on it. Nick was letting out some pretty big moans, and I leaned over and pulled his shirt off and started sucking on his nipples.

When I saw Tony get up off his knees and more into the doggy position, I knew I needed to get behind him. I pulled his shorts and briefs off of him, exposing that perfect round ass. He had absolutely no body hair, and his hole was pristine. I spit on my hand to get my finger wet and started rubbing in on his hole. He never even flinched and kept sucking on Nick's cock. I leaned forward and slowly started to kiss his cheeks before rolling my tongue into his tight hole. Just as I did this, he arched his back like a cat, and I knew he liked it.

I buried my face as deep in his ass as I could for a few more minutes before Nick said he wanted to taste it. He pulled Tony up on the couch so that he was standing over Nick and kind of crouching down with his ass in his face. I could see his long tongue going right into Tony's ass. Nick's cock was kind of bouncing around while he was eating Tony's ass, so I crawled forward and grabbed a hold of it and started sucking on the head. I was stroking it while I was sucking it because I knew that's exactly how Nick liked it. In between tongue thrusts, I could hear both Nick and Tony letting out loud moans.

This went on for a few more minutes before Nick told Tony it was time to sit on his dick. I got up to go grab the lube, and when I came back into the office, Tony was already riding him. Nick must have really gotten his hole soaking wet. He was riding Nick's cock with his knees bent and only his feet holding him up, and Nick was grabbing onto his ass to kind of assist. I pulled my pants the rest of the way off and stood over Nick facing Tony so that he could suck my cock. Tony grabbed onto my dick and shoved it into his mouth, and then I felt Nick's tongue slip into my hole. I had one hand on the back of Tony's head while it bobbed back and forth on my wet dick, and my other hand on the back of Nick's head pulling his face closer into my ass.

I wanted to get a piece of Tony's ass, too, so I said it was my turn and hopped off the couch. I went behind Tony and kind of pulled him off of Nick's cock and pushed him forward a little bit, so he was leaning over Nick's shoulder. Nick grabbed Tony's ass and spread it open for me while I lubed up my cock, and that thing slid right into his loose hole. I grabbed onto his hips and fucked him as hard as I could, and I could tell he liked it. Nick was kissing Tony's shoulder and neck, and I could see him reaching down and grabbing for his cock to jerk him off. Fucking his hole after Nick kind of sucked because Nick really had loosened him up.

I fucked him for a few more minutes before saying it was time to DP. I pulled out of his hole so that he could sit back on Nick's dick, which slid in with no problem. Tony started bouncing up and down, and while he did, I poured lube down his crack and pushed it into his hole with my finger. I put extra lube on my cock and pressed the head of it against Tony's hole, just above Nick's cock. I was able to get the head in with no problem, and Tony was moaning louder than I had heard earlier. I let the head sit there for a minute, and when Tony started moving his ass back and forth a little bit, I started pushing more of my rod into his ass.

It took a few minutes, but my entire shaft was all the way in his hole with Nick's. I thrusted just a little bit because I knew between the friction of our dicks inside his ass, that I was going to blow my load pretty quickly. I love the feeling of my cock rubbing against Nick's, and I kept catching Nick staring at me rather than at Tony. I was almost as if he didn't even know Tony was there with us. Tony arched his back and leaned toward me so he could kiss me, and Nick leaned forward and started kissing his chest. Not much time had passed, and I started blowing my load deep in his hole. Just as I did, I could feel Nick's cock start to throb, and I knew he was blowing his load too. That, and he let out his loud orgasmic screech. We both pumped our cum deep into Tony's hole, and then I slowly pulled my cock out before Nick did. When my dick popped out, so did a shit ton of cum.

Tony got off of Nick's dick and sat next to him on the couch and started stroking his dick. I knelt down in front of him and stuck a few fingers in his ass to help and started sucking on his balls. Nick leaned down and started sucking on his shaft, and not even ten seconds later, Tony yelled out that he was going to cum. We let Tony grab his dick and stroke his load out, both of us eagerly waiting to catch his warm load in our mouths.

This kid could shoot a fucking load like no other. He got so much in my mouth that I actually had to close it, so I didn't gag, and he still covered half my face. Same with Nick. Nick turned to me, and we started making out, and it was like getting a second load to the face. I swallowed what was in my mouth and wiped off with a towel. I told Tony he could shower if he wanted, but he said he wanted to keep our loads in his ass as long as he could.

We all grabbed our clothes and put them back on. As we were walking toward the front of the office, Tony grabbed the door handle and turned around and looked me. "Thanks, Doc. You and Nick have obviously done this before."

My jaw dropped, and Tony ran out the door. Nick turned and looked at me before leaving. "Round 2?" I just started laughing and told him to get the hell out.

Chapter 3

JACOB

After the last few days that I had in the office, I knew I needed a break. Rocky was just about finished with this schooling, so I decided to let him handle a few of my patients who were looking to pay less for a session. Although, with Rocky in the session, I knew they would get the same kind of treatment that I would offer them.

I decided to head down to a local park for the day and do some kayaking. Some alone time in nature was always good for me and always helped me wind down after a whirlwind few days. Because it was the middle of the week, the park was creepily empty. I loaded my kayak into the water and started rowing down the river.

This park was a known gay cruising spot, especially during the week because of how empty it was. I kept looking from side to side to see if I could spot any action happening. About 10 minutes into my journey, I spotted two guys in the bushes messing around, and they weren't making any attempt to hide it. I could actually hear them before I saw them. It was two big burly men going at it doggy style. I stopped paddling so I could watch for just a minute as I floated by and started getting a boner. I was rubbing on my cock through my shorts as I was floating and kind of hoped they would see me and wave me to join them, but that was wishful thinking. My kayak eventually floated past them where I lost sight, and I kept rowing again.

About a mile down the river was a little park that had a shelter, a small beach, and some showers. There was always a lot of activity there because of the showers, so I decided to get out of the river and just relax for a little bit. I sat down in the pavilion and opened up one of my apps to see if there was anyone nearby. I was feeling a bit horny after seeing the guys in the bushes and wanted to get a little action. I thought maybe they would check their phones and want a little more.

There was a guy named Jacob active, and it said he was about 25 feet away from me. I stood up and looked around but didn't see any cars or anyone in the area. I figured he had to have been in one of the bathrooms or showers, so I decided to go scope it out and see if I could find him.

I walked into the first set of showers, but it was silent. There were two different buildings that housed showers—one for men and one for women. The women one was basically only used for cruising. I didn't think he would be in that one alone, but I figured I'd check it out.

I opened the door to the building and could hear the water running. I walked through slowly until I could figure out which stall he was in. I leaned against the wall and saw one with the shower curtain about a fourth of the way open. That was always the sign that someone wanted to be caught. I couldn't see his entire body but could tell he was leaning his back against the wall and slowly stroking his cock. I started rubbing mine again through my shorts, which quickly grew to a full, hard eight inches.

He turned around and purposely hit the shower curtain, opening it up a little more. I took my shirt off, pushed my shorts off, and walked over to the shower stall. He turned around and looked at me, still stroking his massive monster. I walked into the stall, cock rock hard, and leaned against the wall. We both stood there for a few minutes, staring into each other's eyes and stroking our pieces, and then he dropped down to his knees in front of me and opened his mouth. I put my hand on the back of his head and guided him toward me, and I could feel the head of my penis press through to the back of his throat. He went the entire way down my shaft before closing his mouth and then slowly came back up, releasing it from his mouth.

I grabbed onto my dick and lifted it so he would move down to my balls, and he started sucking on them while I was stroking. He grabbed onto my leg a propped it up so he could have access to my hole and dug his way into it with his tongue. He had his head back bent and was going deep into my hole with his tongue, and it was honestly the first time I had been eaten like this. I wanted to give him easier access, so I turned around and leaned against the wall, arching my back with my ass right in his face. He grabbed onto my cheeks and spread them apart, giving him free range to me. He dove back inside of my with his tongue, which must have been as long as his cock was.

I let him go to town for a few minutes before turning around and dropping down to my knees in front of him. He was still on his knees, and I grabbed onto his face and started making out with him. The water was still pouring all over us the entire time, and it was actually a really hot experience. I pushed him back so he was sitting down and leaning against the wall and leaned down in front of him so I could start sucking on his monster. I could barely get the entire thing in my mouth but did the best I could. Not only was it long, but he was pretty girthy as well. I sucked and stroked on that thing for about 30 seconds but couldn't resist any longer, and wanted him inside of me.

I stood up and turned around, leaning against the wall again. I didn't even have to say anything—he knew what I wanted. I spit on my hand and rubbed it over my hole while he did the same to his cock. He grabbed onto my hips while I guided his cock inside of me. Even without lube, and even with his massive size, he had no problem easing his way in. He didn't give me any time to adjust and just started pounding my ass, never letting go of my hips. I leaned back at one point so we could kiss but quickly turned back toward the wall, hanging onto the railing for dear life while he tore me up.

He only lasted for about two minutes before I could feel him start pounding harder and faster, and I knew he was going to blow. I started stroking on my cock as fast as I could so we could cum at the same time, and just as I started blowing my load on the wall of the shower, he let out a loud moan and a final hard thrust, and I could feel him exploding inside of me.

He pumped that load deep inside of me with a few final thrusts before letting himself slide out of my ass. I was still leaning against the wall, and he got down behind me and started licking the cum from my ass, diving his tongue in as deep as he could. I turned around and shoved my cock in his mouth, allowing him to get the rest of what was dripping from my head.

He got out of the shower while I stayed in and turned around and smiled.

"Thanks. I'm Jacob, by the way."

I was a bit in shock by what had just happened and couldn't find the words to respond, so I just waved at him, knowing I'd be coming back to that park very soon.

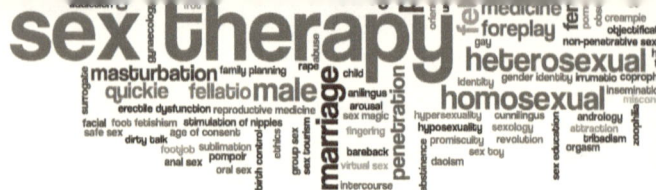

Chapter 4

JACOB PART 2

I decided to take the following day as an office day. I really needed to catch up on my files and really couldn't afford any interruptions. I had planned on going back to the park that night after work if I could get all of my charts done, hoping to run into Jacob again.

A few hours after I got to the office, I heard someone knocking at the door. It wasn't really all that often that people would come knocking on my door as it clearly said, "Appointments Required." I used to take walk-ins but couldn't handle the influx anymore. I ignored the knocking, but the person wasn't going away. I walked up front and opened the blinds and was shocked at who it was.

Jacob.

I wasn't sure if it was just a coincidence that he was there or if he somehow knew who I was. I opened up the door and he walked right in.

"Hey, Jacob. Umm. I'm not really sure what's going on."

He looked at me and smiled. "It's my turn to feel you inside of me."

I shut the door and locked it, and I had barely even turned around before he was pushing me against the wall to kiss me. We made out for quite a while, right on the couch in my lobby, and I popped a boner within seconds. We made our way over to the couch. He was lying on top of me while we were making out, and I could feel his dick rubbing against mine. Jacob would slide his hands down my chest and rub my boner through my pants, and then he would come back up and grab my face. He was a passionate kisser, just like he was the day before.

We both stood up from the couch and I tore his clothes off of him as fast as I could and turned him around, so he was facing the wall. I took my own clothes off and started kissing his neck as I was rubbing my cock on his ass, teasing his hole with the tip of my head.

I grabbed his hand so we could make our way back to my therapy room. The couch was much bigger and that's where my lube was. He pushed me against the door and dropped down and started sucking on my dick. I grabbed the back of his head, thrusting my cock as deep into his mouth as I could. I was still shocked that he could take the entire thing without a single gag. He sucked on it for a while and then stood up and asked if I liked eating ass. I didn't even answer.

I turned him around and pushed him down on the couch and dove right into his ass. He was so smooth, and I could tell he spent a while cleaning his hole because it tasted so fresh and so good. I swirled my tongue around the edge of his hole and then slowly started licking on top of it. I spread his cheeks with my hands and slowly pushed my tongue inside, twirling it around as it went in and out. He was thrusting his hips back and forth, and I could tell he was enjoying himself.

I reached into the drawer and grabbed the lube while I was still eating his hole. He was still laying on his stomach with his ass perched up, so once I was lubed up, I shoved my dick in without any hesitation and started going to pound town on his ass. I wasn't sure if he was really more of a top or a bottom, but I took it pretty rough on him. I grabbed onto his hips and forced myself against him, going back and forth, pushing my cock inside his hole as hard as I could.

I grabbed his legs and flipped him around on his back without letting my dick come out. I put his legs over my shoulders and started fucking him again as he just kept saying, "Harder, harder." He grabbed onto his hard dick and started stroking as fast as he could, and within a minute, he was shooting his load all over his chest, and even up to his face. Seeing this was a huge turn on for me, so I pulled my cock out and got up and strattled his face, stroking my tool until I exploded, shooting my load straight down his throat. I knew he liked the taste of cum based on what had happened yesterday. I wanted to cum on his face but noticed he was opening his mouth, so I knew he wanted to swallow it, and I was more than willing to give it to him.

He took every drop of cum, and when I was done shooting, he leaned forward to make sure he sucked every last drop out of my dick. He got up and grabbed my notebook and wrote his number down. He then said that he'd be at the showers tomorrow with a few friends, and I knew exactly where I would be spending my next evening.

Chapter 5

RYAN RETURNS

*T*he next morning, Rocky came running into my room and asked why I wasn't in the office. I thought he had cancelled all of my meetings for the rest of the week, but he said I had received a last-minute request for a new patient, and that he accepted it because he figured I would want to meet this patient. I was kind of pissed because I really just needed some time to relax, but I also didn't want to cancel on a new patient.

I went into the office and started working on some charts while I waited for the new patient to arrive. He didn't show up at his scheduled time, but I wasn't fully paying attention because I was so far behind on my charts. After about two hours, I decided I was just going to head home and finish the day there. As I was walking toward the front of the office, the door swung open, and I couldn't believe my eyes.

It was Ryan—one of the guys who had fucked me in Ireland.

"Heeeyyyyy. Uh. What are you doing here?" I couldn't help but admire his gorgeous body.

"I haven't been able to stop thinking about you since the night Scott brought you home from the pub. I had the opportunity to come over to LA for work, and I saw one of your advertisements at a club in West Hollywood and decided to come up for the day to see you."

I was in shock seeing him standing in front of me. Honestly, I really hadn't thought about him. The only thing I really remembered from my trip was the sex house in Prague. Everything else was miniscule compared to that portion of my trip.

I asked him if he wanted to go grab some coffee, but he shook his head and said he only had about two hours before he needed to head back to the airport. I walked around him and pushed the door shut and locked it.

"Okay then. Follow me."

I grabbed his hand, and he followed me back to my therapy room. I knew what he wanted, and I hoped that this time he would let me fuck him. He entered the room, sat down on the couch, and waved for me to come toward him. I walked over to him and straddled his lap, wrapping my arms around the back of his head. He held onto my hips and pulled me closer to his chest and leaned forward to start kissing me. He moved down and started sucking on my neck and quickly pulled my shirt off. I started unbuttoning his shirt while we were making out and realized how passionate of a kisser he was.

We made out for a solid 15 minutes before he lifted me off of him and laid me down on the couch with my head on the armrest. He slid on top of me, rubbing his body against mine as he came back up to my face to start kissing me again. I moved my hands down his back and into his pants, grabbing onto his ass, and realized that I really did want to fuck him. I pulled him close into me, feeling his hard tool rub against mine. He leaned up and grabbed the waistband of my pants, pulling them completely off. He came back down and started rubbing his chin against my briefs, gently licking my cock on top of my underwear.

I pulled my underwear down, and he grabbed them and threw them on the floor. He dove in between my legs and started licking just below my balls, sucking on them and then working his way up, licking up my shaft and to the head of my dick before opening his mouth and swallowing the entire thing. He slipped his finger into my hole while he was sucking on my cock, slobbering all over it and getting me completely wet. He was moving up and down, fast for a few moments, and then slow, teasing the head before taking the entire thing again.

He got up and took his pants off before crawling back up to me, my head still on the arm rest. He was straddling my chest, stroking his dick right in front of my face, and I grabbed his hips to pull him closer so I could devour his monster. He grabbed the back of my head and held on tight so that his cock was pressing against the back of my throat. He held it there for a few seconds, completely gagging me before letting it free from my mouth. I was drooling all over, and I quickly took that thing back in and started stroking it while I was sucking on it.

He saw the lube sitting on the table, grabbed it, and lubed up my cock while I was still swallowing his, and I knew exactly what he wanted. He backed himself away from my face, still straddling me, and lowered his ass down on my piece. He must have been a bottom, because he took no time sitting on it and letting the entire thing inside of him—no time to adjust—and just started bouncing up and down as fast as he could. His hole felt so good wrapped around my dick, and I grabbed onto his back and pulled his head forward, so I could kiss him and take control.

We started making out and I perched him up so I could be in control, thrusting my body into his ass as fast and hard as I could. I knew I wasn't going to last very long, and within two minutes felt myself getting close. I pushed him back up so I could grab onto his cock and start stroking it, and within seconds, he was shooting his load all over my chest. The moment I saw his thick batter on me, I started exploding in his hole, letting out a loud moan.

He rubbed his fingers in his cum all over my chest and fed it to me, leaning down to make out some more and swap the load a little bit. Once my dick fell out of his hole, he moved down toward the end of the couch and started sucking on it. I don't know how, but he got me fully hard again and had me blowing another load in his mouth in less than two minutes, swallowing every last drop.

He looked at the clock on the wall and jumped up off the couch. "I'm going to miss my flight." He gave me a kiss on the cheek and told me to come visit him again, and I grabbed my phone and immediately started looking for flights.

Chapter 6

THE SHOWERS

I had every intention on just spending the rest of the day at home, but as soon as I walked in the door, I received a notification on my phone from one of my apps. It was from Jacob.

"Showers—8pm." With what had just happened at my office with Ryan, I had totally forgotten that Jacob said he and his friends were going to the showers at the park, and I definitely wanted a hot, steamy night again. Instead of kayaking to the showers, I figured I would just park and walk because it would be much easier, and my arms wouldn't get tired, just in case I needed them for anything.

I could see that the lights were on in the showers, and since the park was closed after dark, I knew everyone had already arrived. There were four cars in the parking lot, so there were at least four guys, including Jacob inside. When I opened the door to walk in, there were five guys all sitting on the benches, already naked, stroking their cocks and laughing.

Jacob ran up to me and gave me a hug and a kiss and then whispered in my ear, "They all want your ass." That's when I realized this wasn't going to be the typical orgy where you just take any dick or hole within reach. I was going to be the center of attention.

Jacob quickly pulled my pants down while I took my shirt off and then pushed me down on the ground in front of him, aiming his massive monster right in my face. I gladly accepted, opening my mouth and swallowing as much as I could. I noticed the four other guys stand up and all move toward me, forming a circle around me. I grabbed onto the guy's dicks who were on either side of Jacob and started stroking both of them as I was sucking on Jacob, and then slowly moved around the circle, sucking on each cock for a while before moving onto the next.

With a cock in my mouth, I could feel fingers and tongues going in and out of my hole but had no clue who it was. All of the guys were pretty well endowed, and I knew what was going to happen next.

I was back to sucking on Jacob's dick when I felt someone shove theirs straight inside of me, wasting no time before pounding away. I was in a little bit of pain, but also a bit of euphoria at the same time. He fucked me for about a minute before pulling out and letting the next guy in.

The guys would switch off every few minutes like a revolving door with the ones waiting to enter me pushing their cocks into my mouth. I had my eyes close the majority of the time, so I really didn't know who was doing what until Jacob got inside of my hole, a cock I definitely wouldn't forget.

One of the guys whose dick I was sucking on pulled out of my mouth and sat down against the wall in front of me, pulling me toward him and forcing Jacob's cock to pull out of my ass. The guy pulled me against him so that I was riding his dick, and then pulled my body forward and over him so that Jacob could come up behind me and get inside too. This was a lot different than when I was DP'd in Ireland as these guys dicks were way thicker.

It took Jacob a minute to get fully inside of me, and my body froze for a minute in pain, hoping my hole could adjust to what was happening. I felt Jacob slowly start moving while the other guy just held on tight, knowing that it was hurting me a bit. Another guy came over and spit on my hole, and I assume stuck his tongue out on Jacob's dick as he was going in and out, and the extra spit helped a little bit, and eventually I was able to start jiving with them.

The other guys were standing around us jerking off, and I could feel them cumming on my back, although I couldn't tell how many did. Within two minutes of being DP'd, I could feel both of them unleashing inside of my hole, everyone grunting and moaning the entire time. Jacob pulled his cock out and bent down to start eating my ass while the other guy was still inside of me.

One of the last guys who still hadn't cum yet pulled me up and put me on my back in front of him, lifting my legs and shoving his dick in my hole. He gave my ass about three pumps before I could feel him flooding my insides, then pulled out and kept jerking off all over my chest.

I was still laying on my back, rock hard, and started stroking my cock. Jacob got down in front of my and lifted my legs to keep eating my ass, and two of the guys came down and started taking turns sucking on my dick. It didn't take long before I was blowing my load all over their faces, and the other guys joined in, licking it off of them.

Before I knew it, all of the guys except Jacob had disappeared. Jacob and I jumped into one of the showers together, cleaning up and making out a little bit, but nothing else happened. As we were putting our clothes on, he asked me if I wanted to grab a drink sometime, and I told him that I'd get ahold of him through the app.

We never talked again.

Chapter 7

AUSTIN

I spent the next few days really catching up at work and seeing patients. I actually had a lot of new patients coming in and decided to make a rule that patients had to see me three times before getting one of my "special sessions." It was just getting way too hard to keep up and manage the scheduling with constantly having to cancel, so I was going to just have to have certain days where those sessions took place. I knew I needed to hire additional therapists, so I had Rocky place an ad online so we could start screening candidates.

That Friday night on my way home, I got a notification on one of my apps. It was from this really hot guy named Austin. His first message was typical: "You're really cute." All guys usually started off with that type of message, but from his pictures, he seemed like a really down-home type of guy. And then his next message came through. "How big's your dick?" I just laughed a little bit.

"Wow, you really get right to the point, don't you?" I responded to him. He then responded with a picture of his cock, and I immediately got hard because it was probably the most beautiful dick I had ever seen.

"This is an app. I'm not looking to get married on here haha." He responded to me. And he was right. This was a hook-up app. Of course, I had always hoped I would meet the love of my life on here, even though 99% of guys were just on here looking for action.

We talked non-stop for several days with some heavy flirting. He would even call and face-time me, and one night after work, I was doing some shopping, and he was begging for me to come over. I really didn't want to because I knew we'd end up in bed together, and I had just eaten fast food, worked out on my lunch, and hadn't taken a shower. But he convinced me, and next thing I knew, I was pulling into his driveway.

He came running down off the front porch and gave me a huge hug. He had music playing and drinks already poured. We were talking and singing and just having a really good time. Out of nowhere, he turned toward me on the couch and just started making out with me with everyone in the neighborhood able to watch us. He started rubbing his hand on my cock and trying to pull it out to suck on it, but I wouldn't let him because I hadn't showered. He pulled his shorts down and whipped it out, and it was even bigger and prettier than the picture made it.

I pushed him on his back and got down in front of him and took the entire thing in my mouth, bobbing my head up and down. I could tell we were just messing around and neither of us were ready for the full thing, so I quickly got up and started dancing on the porch, and he pulled his shorts back up and joined me. We were just having a genuinely good time.

We went inside to the kitchen and took the music with us, making more drinks and playing our favorite songs. I was sitting on the counter, and he kept coming up to me and giving me little kisses. For someone who wanted to know my dick size and didn't want to get married, he was extremely flirtatious. For a moment I actually thought to myself—this might be the guy.

We made our way into his bedroom, and I told him I wanted to take a shower. I jumped in the shower, and a minute later, he followed me in. He dropped down to his knees and swallowed my cock, sucking on it with the water running over us, making me rock hard. He stood up and grabbed the conditioner, rubbed it all over my dick and turned around and bent over, guiding me inside of him. I immediately grabbed onto his hips and started pumping. His hole felt amazing, but I didn't want to finish like this, so I gave him a few pumps and then pulled out. He turned around, and I got down and started sucking on his dick. He grabbed my face, and I looked up at him and told him to spit in my mouth. He did, and then I kept on sucking on his dick.

We got out of the shower, and I jumped into bed. He grabbed his phone and smiled and asked if I wanted to record it. Normally I would have said no, but I felt oddly safe with him, so I agreed. He propped his phone up on the TV and then jumped into bed with me. We were under the covers and started passionately kissing, rubbing our hands all over each other's bodies. This felt so different than anything else I had encountered before. I could have kissed this guy for hours and not even do anything else.

I ran my hands all over his body, grabbing his cock and stroking it, feeling his hole, rubbing my hands up his back and through his flowing golden hair. He was an absolutely amazing kisser.

I pushed him off of me and started kissing his neck, making my way down his chiseled chest and letting that massively hard cock enter my mouth. I had to grab onto the base and stroke it while I was sucking it because of its size. I would have been happy just sucking on that thing and not even doing anything else. There was just something about its perfect size, and even the way it looked, that just drew me to it.

I turned my body around so we could 69 and lowered my hole right onto his tongue while slobbing on his knob. He pushed me over onto my side so he could suck on my dick, and we went to town on each other, grabbing each other's heads and sucking as hard as we could.

I needed to feel him inside of me. I asked him if he had any lube, which I then noticed was already on the nightstand along with some poppers. I grabbed the lube, moistened up his cock, and laid down in front of him. He lifted my legs while I sniffed on the poppers and guided his monster inside of me. Even with its size, I was so horny that it just glided right in. I held the poppers up to him so he could take a sniff, and he leaned down and started making out with me while beginning to thrust his hips.

He kissed me the entire time he was fucking me with his cock going in and out nice and slowly. It actually felt more like we were making love than just fucking, and I didn't want either of us to cum because I wanted this to last as long as possible. After a few minutes, I told him to get on top of me. He pulled out and lubed up my dick, sitting down on it and bouncing for his dear life. His dick was big enough that I could suck on it while fucking him, which was making him start to moan. I let his cock fall out of my mouth and grabbed his head, pulling him down and kissing him while moving my body with his. It was as if we were in true alignment. He sat up, stopped moving, looked at me, and smiled. "I have an idea."

He got up from on top of me and ran over to his closet and grabbed this black machine. I couldn't quite tell what it was until he sat it down on the nightstand. It was a fucking machine—the type that you attached a dildo to and let it fuck you. I had never used one of these before, but I was intrigued.

He sat it up and attached a fairly thick dildo and then pulled me over to the edge of the bed. I propped my legs up on the nightstand while he inserted the dildo in my hole, and then turned it on. That machine immediately started pounding me, and I couldn't believe how real it felt. How had I never used one of these before? He turned it on a little faster and then leaned down and started sucking on my cock while the machine was fucking me. He grabbed onto the base of my dick and was stroking it while slobbing all over it, and after a minute, he got back on top and started riding me again.

I absolutely love getting fucked and fucking at the same time. It was a bit of an awkward position to be ridden while hanging off the edge of the bed, but I held us up with my legs and just hung on tight. He was bouncing with the same rhythm as the machine, and it felt fucking amazing.

I could feel myself getting close and still wasn't ready to cum, so I told him that it was his turn on the machine. We switched places, and I started sucking on his dick while the machine was fucking him. I wanted to feel him inside of me again, so I turned the machine off, and he got back into a normal position on the bed so I could ride him. My balls were rubbing against his rock-hard chest as he grabbed onto my ass and pounded away, and I swear my eyes were rolling into the back of my head. I rode him hard for a few minutes and then got off and lifted his legs so I could start fucking him again. We were so horned up we didn't even need to re-lube when flipping around.

I grabbed one of the dildos on the table and pushed it into his hole while I was fucking him, and he let out a loud scream. I leaned down forward and started kissing him again, letting go of the dildo so I could touch him. I knew I was about to cum and started pumping as hard and fast as I could until I exploded in his hole, still pumping until every last drop was inside of him. I knew he was ready to cum, so I got up and started riding his dick again, him leaning forward and licking all of the cum off my cock. I was bouncing on him as hard as I could when I felt him give one final thrust. I could feel his load flooding my hole, and I told him to keep fucking as hard as he could.

I leaned down, and we started making out again, rolling around on the bed and kissing for another 15 minutes. We took a shower and then hopped back into bed, cuddling and falling asleep. We must have woken up four or five times throughout the night, fucking each time, with each time being even better than the last.

This is it, I thought. *This is the guy I've been looking for.*

I ended up spending the entire weekend with him. We never even left his bedroom, and I couldn't even tell you how many times we fucked.

This went on for over a year with Austin. We never officially said we were in a relationship, but you couldn't separate us. That is, until the video went viral.

One morning when I was at home, I woke up to over a hundred text messages. The first one I opened was from Rocky, and it was a link to a porn website. I clicked on it and couldn't believe what I was watching.

It was the video that we had made the first time we met.

I tried calling Austin, but he wouldn't answer. Never in my life had I imagined that he would have posted the video, and it was going viral, probably due to the title: "My night with Dr. Cage."

The video already had over five million views, and I knew there was nothing I could do about it. I knew the news would spread and my parents would find out about it, and I was afraid that this could possibly impact my practice.

I was never able to get ahold of Austin. It was almost as if he had just vanished. It actually made me wonder if he had just used me for the video. But why would he wait a year to post it? Everything we had seemed so real.

I went into the office that morning to find Rocky was already there. He was behind the computer and looked completely frazzled.

"Hunter, umm, we better hire these other therapists ASAP. Because of your video, we just had 500 requests for new patient sessions."

And with that video, I became famous.

Author Bio

Grayson Ace has had his fair share of sexcapades, and figured why not write about them? Recently divorced, he is re-discovering himself (and plenty of hot men) and creating many new sexy adventures along the way. If you like what you see, please leave a review, and you never know....you may end up in one of the stories!

GraysonAce.com
Facebook: Grayson Ace
Instagram: graysonaceofficial
Twitter: @GraysonAce1

4 Horsemen Publications

LGBT Erotica

Leo Sparx
Before Alexander
Claiming Alexander
Taming Alexander
Saving Alexander

Erotica

Ali Whippe
Office Hours
Tutoring Center
Athletics
Extra Credit
Bound for Release
Fetish Circuit

Dalia Lance
My Home on Whore Island
Slumming It on Slut Street
Training of the Tramp
The Imperfect Perfection
72% Match
It Was Meant To Be... Or Whatever

4HorsemenPublications.com

www.ingramcontent.com/pod-product-compliance
Lightning Source LLC
Chambersburg PA
CBHW050501110726
47899CB00003B/1026

* 9 7 8 1 6 4 4 5 0 6 3 5 6 *